The
MUSIC
STORE

and Other Stories

NEIL BLACKFIELD

STARTING GATE • BOOK FIVE

International Standard Book Number: 1-57128-112-6

10 09 08 07
0 9 8 7 6 5

High Noon Books
a division of ATP
20 Commercial Boulevard
Novato, California 94949-6191

Table of Contents

Note to Teachers and Parents

These stories were written to give the new reader success in reading. They use words from a 315-word vocabulary list.

Because the vocabulary is cumulative, students should read the books in order. Before the student attempts to read the first story in Book 1, she or he should know by sight (be able to read out loud) all of the "101 Words to Read," which are listed at the back of Book 1.

Have the student copy each of the "101 Words to Read" on a 3" by 5" card, and then learn the words by whatever method the instructor or student chooses.

The same method should be used with the "New Word" list given for each story.

In addition, help the student with the names of the characters, such as "Tony" or "Sally," in the story during the first reading.

A phonics program of your choice should be used by the student along with the stories.

The Music Store

New Words

band	kind
different	music
drums	right
few	sound
hurry	start

The Music Store

Max wanted to play the drums. His friend Jane was starting a band, and Max wanted to be in the band. He knew that if he wanted to, he could learn how to play the drums. He had a friend who played the drums. Her name was Mary, and she said she would teach him how to play the drums. Max wanted to play the drums and be in Jane's band. Mary told Max he could come to her house and play her drums until he got some of his own. Max and Mary were very good friends, and he knew that Mary would help him learn how to play the drums.

A few days went by, and Mary asked Max if he wanted her to go to the music store with him to look at some drums. Max wanted to go to the music store and look at drums, and he was happy that Mary wanted to go with him. Mary knew a lot about the different kinds of drums at the music store. Mary would be able to tell Max all about the different drums and help him pick out the right drums.

The music store was a big place. It had many different kinds of drums. Max wanted to look at all the drums. He wanted to be a drummer, and he knew he could do it. Jane wanted to start her band right away, so Max was in a hurry to get some drums. Jane wanted Max to be in the band, and all he needed was to get some drums.

One of the people who worked in the store came over to ask Mary and Max if they needed any help with the drums. Mary knew what would be good for Max, so they did not need to talk with the music store worker for very long. Max was very happy that he had Mary with him, and Mary was very happy to be able to help Max.

After talking with Mary, Max took some drums home with him. He was very happy with his new drums. They sounded very good to him when he played them.

He played them every day, and Jane knew that she was going to have a very good drummer for her new band. Mary said she would come see the new band play and help Max if he needed any more help. Mary was a good friend of Max's, and this made his day.

The Post Office

New Words

behind	holidays
card	mind
chance	post
counter	ready
front	send

The Post Office

The holidays were coming.
Maria wanted to do
something nice for her
friends. She wanted to send
holiday cards to her friends.
Maria knew that her friends
would like to get holiday
cards in the mail. Maria
could make her holiday

cards on her computer. Maria had made other things on her computer, so she knew she could make the cards. After making her holiday cards, she could go to the post office and mail them to her friends.

Maria made her holiday cards on her computer. Before her cards could be mailed, Maria would have to

put stamps on them. Maria
knew that she could buy
some stamps at the post
office. The post office would
not mail Maria's cards if
they did not have stamps
on them. Maria took her
holiday cards and got in her
car to go to the post office.

When Maria got to the
post office, there were other
people there. She had to

wait in a very long line.
Maria did not mind because
she could visit with the
other people in the line at
the post office. She knew
some of the people in the
line, and she was happy to
talk to them. Sometimes the
line at the post office is very
long, and you have a lot of
time to talk with your friends
and other people.

When Maria got to the front of the line, the post office worker behind the counter was ready to talk with her. Maria wanted to know how much money she would need to buy her stamps. The post office worker was happy to tell her how much money she would need to buy the stamps. Maria gave the post office worker the money, and she got her stamps. She could now send her holiday cards to her friends.

After the holidays Maria was happy to learn that all her friends got her holiday cards. Her friends were very happy to get the cards from Maria. Maria was very happy with the post office.

They did a good job with her cards. She knew that the post office was the right place to go to send her cards and letters to all of her friends. She would use the post office again.

The New Library

New Words

able	library
book	open
hold	read
information	together
Internet	use

The New Library

The new library was about to open. Tim was very happy that the new library was about to open. He knew that there would be new books to read as well as new computers to help him with his work. Tim did not have a new computer at his house, but he knew he could use the new computers at the new library. He had read in the newspaper that the computers at the new library would let him use the Internet too.

Tim went to visit the new library. He wanted to get a new book to read about fixing cars. Tim liked to

work on cars, and he liked
to help his friends fix their
cars. The book he wanted
was not in the library at this
time. He would have to
place a "hold" on the book
he wanted. Tim knew from
other libraries that he would
be able to use one of the
new computers at the new
library to place a "hold" on a
book. The library would

send him a card in the mail when his book came in to the new library. Tim was very happy that he had a new library in his city with new books for him to read.

Now that Tim was at the library, he was ready to use the Internet on the new computers. Tim knew that he could use the Internet to find information about many different things. He knew that the Internet was many different computers working together. By using the Internet, Tim could look at the things and information that other people had put on their computers all over the place.

Tim, from the Internet computer at the library, could look up information that was on computers in many different cities. Tim could do all of this and find new information, too, by using the new Internet computers at the library.

Tim was surprised to learn that he would not need to use any of his money to look at the information on the Internet. This was because many

different people had put
the information on their
computers for all people to
use, not just for the people
who had money.

Tim had a good day at
the library. He was able to
place a "hold" on a book he
wanted, and he got to use
the new Internet computer.
He knew he would be back
to look for more information

from the books and all the computers working together on the Internet.

City Hall

New Words

also

children

enjoy

family

hall

mayor

raise

tell

thank

thought

City Hall

Maria and Dan were very happy with the people who ran their city. These people thought there should be more parks in their city, and Maria and Dan thought so, too. Dan and Maria knew that they should talk to the people at their city hall and tell them what a nice job they were doing. Not many people would take the time to do that. They would tell them how much they enjoyed being able to use the parks in their city. They would tell them that their children also enjoyed playing in the city parks.

When Maria and Dan got to city hall, they needed to

find the right people to talk to about the parks. They knew that they could ask the city worker behind the information counter. The city worker would know the right people to talk to about the parks. They wanted to tell them how much they enjoyed using the parks in their city.

They wanted to thank the

people who worked to get more money for more parks for their city. Dan and Maria knew that their city was a good place to raise a family because of the nice parks.

After talking with the worker behind the city hall information counter, Maria and Dan knew they should go and talk to the mayor of the city.

The mayor of the city could tell the other city workers that Dan and Maria wanted to thank them for the good job they were doing with the city parks. The mayor would know all the people who worked for their city and would know how to tell them that some nice people (Dan and Maria) were pleased with the job that the people who worked for the city were doing.

Maria and Dan talked with the mayor. She thought it would be nice for them to send a card of thanks to the city workers. The mayor then could take the card and show it to all the city workers. The park workers would then know that the people of the city liked the job they were doing with the parks in the city.

Dan and Maria went to the store and got a very nice card to send to the mayor and the city workers. They were happy to send the card as they wanted to give a big "thank you" to their city for making the parks a good place to visit and a nice place to play for all of the children.

101 Words to Read

a	came	have
about	can	he
all	come	her
am	could	here
an	did	him
and	do	his
any	find	how
are	for	I
as	from	if
at	get	in
away	go	into
be	good	is
been	got	it
before	had	know
but	happy	laugh
by	has	like

little	please	us
look	ran	very
made	run	want
make	said	was
may	saw	we
me	say	went
my	see	were
new	she	when
no	so	where
not	some	which
now	that	who
of	the	will
on	them	with
or	then	would
our	there	yes
out	they	you
over	this	your
play	to	

Word List

Book One

bake	house	teacher
bed	job	their
big	lab	time
black	lunch	walk
boss	mall	white
buy	market	work
cake	road	workers
car	sandwich	
cheese	school	
chicken	sell	## Book Two
computer	shoe	
day	sit	air
down	sky	apple
eat	stand	bird
food	store	boat
friend	street	build
from	student	cut
fruit	sun	duck
grill	talk	fix

fresh	ride	anymore
hello	sail	back
help	should	because
just	side	better
knew	small	big
lake	television	birthday
learn	too	call
letter	took	could
luck	tree	dinner
made	until	end
mail	watch	family
many	way	far
need	wear	fast
next	week	find
nice	why	found
orange		gave
park		gone
party	**Book Three**	great
people		hike
place	after	hill
put	airplane	jump

	Book Four	
kind		money
nice		motel
off	after	movies
one	again	mud, muddy
pick	because	museum
place	before	newspaper
reach	children	office
seem	city	other
something	clean	pick
surprise	doctor	popcorn
table	drink	right
telephone	feel	room
three	four	sleep
today	gone	sodas
told	hard	take
two	line	thing
up	list	think
visit	long	tickets
wait	lot	wash
window	magazine	water
	medicine	well